W9-AEY-114

The Giant Ice Cream Mess

Tina
Kügler

ACORN™
SCHOLASTIC INC.

To my editor, Katie, we both had the same first job: professional ice cream scooper! – TK

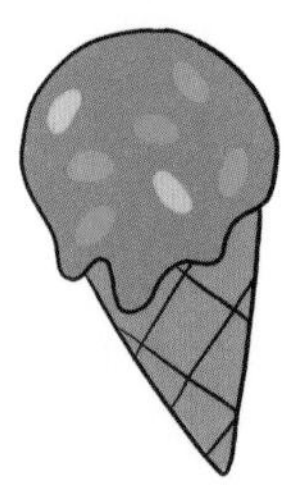

Library of Congress Cataloging-in-Publication Data

Names: Kügler, Tina, author, illustrator. Title: The giant ice cream mess / Tina Kügler.
Description: First edition. | New York : Acorn/Scholastic Inc., 2021. | Series: Fox tails ; 3 | Summary: Competitive fox siblings Fritz and Franny both love ice cream, but when Mr. Bear's ice cream truck stops on their street they spend so much time trying to outdo each other imagining multiple flavors and toppings (while all the other kids are getting their cones) that the only flavor left is marshmallow pickle ripple—and they can only have one scoop each. Identifiers: LCCN 2019059088 | ISBN 9781338561722 (paperback) | ISBN 9781338561746 (library binding) | Subjects: LCSH: Foxes—Juvenile fiction. | Ice cream, ices, etc.—Juvenile fiction. | Ice cream trucks—Juvenile fiction. | Brothers and sisters—Juvenile fiction. | Competition (Psychology)—Juvenile fiction. | CYAC: Ice cream, ices, etc.—Fiction. | Competition (Psychology)—Fiction. | Brothers and sisters—Fiction. | Foxes—Fiction. | Animals—Fiction. Classification: LCC PZ7.1.K844 Gi 2021 | DDC [E]—dc23
LC record available at https://lccn.loc.gov/2019059088

10 9 8 7 6 5 4 3 2 1 21 22 23 24 25

Printed in China 62

First edition, May 2021

Edited by Katie Carella

Book design by Sarah Dvojack

Ding-a-ling!

This is Fritz.

This is Franny.

This is Fred.

I can throw
the ball high.
FOXES

I can throw
the ball higher.

DING-A-LING!
DING-A-LING!

THE ICE CREAM

TRUCK IS COMING!

Hooray!
I love ice cream!
I love ice cream
more than you do!

I want a waffle cone!
I want a waffle cone with sprinkles!

Come and get your ice cream!
Mr. Bear makes the BEST ice cream!
TOPPINGS
SCOOPS
FLAVORS

TOPPINGS
SCOOPS
FLAVORS
1
2
3
I want five kinds of toppings!
I want ten kinds of toppings!

Wow! Look at all the flavors.
SCOOPS
1
2
3

There are so many!

PS FLAVORS
3
Super Duper Vanilla!
Cherry Crunch!
Jelly Bean Swirl!
Blueberry Supreme!
Choco-Chocolate!

Marshmallow Pickle Ripple?
YUCK!

You can each get ONE scoop!
FOXES

Oh No!

I can't pick just one flavor of ice cream.

I want every flavor but Marshmallow Pickle Ripple!
Yuck! Don't even SAY Marshmallow Pickle Ripple!

I want fifty scoops! And twenty toppings!
I want all of that! Plus hot fudge and whipped cream!

Hey! The ice cream truck is gone!
Where did Mr. Bear go?

He went THAT way!

No! He went THIS way!
DING-A-LING!

Look! Mr. Bear is giving Fred a scoop!
It's Marshmallow Pickle Ripple! Poor Fred!

TOPPINGS
SCOOPS
FLAVORS
1
2
3

Hello, Foxes! Would you like a scoop of Marshmallow Pickle Ripple? It is the only flavor I have left.

Oh.

No thank you, Mr. Bear.

TOPPINGS

Bummer. I really wanted ice cream.
Me too.

SLURP!
SLURP! SLURP!

The Best Scoop

TOPPINGS
He does.
He REALLY likes it.

I'll try it
if you try it.

Well, I'll try it if you try it.

One scoop of
Marshmallow Pickle Ripple, please.

PINGS
SCOOPS
FLAVORS
1
2
3

Wow! It's . . . it's . . . good!
This is the BEST ice cream ever!

YUM! Thank you, Mr. Bear!
INGS

Next time I'll bring my new flavor: Bubble Gum Pizza Twist!
BEAR

About the Author

Tina Kügler lives in Los Angeles with her husband and three sons. She loves ice cream so much, she can't even pick one favorite flavor. Her preferred ice cream topping is hot fudge with a spoonful of malted milk powder on top. You should try it sometime!

Tina writes and illustrates books, and also draws cartoons for television. She wrote and illustrated the SNAIL AND WORM beginning reader series and was awarded a Theodor Seuss Geisel Honor in 2018.

Oh, and she also has a cranky lizard named Jabba, a shy cat named Walter Kitty, a cuddly cat named Freddie Purrcury, and a very zippy dog named Lola.

YOU CAN DRAW FRED!

1. Draw an oval for Fred's head.

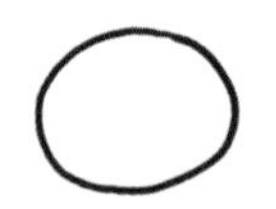

2. Draw a potato shape for his body.

3. Draw Fred's ears, tail, and collar.

4. Draw his spot and four legs. His legs are short!

5. Add all the details. Fred has a big smile and two wrinkles under each eye.

6. Color in your drawing!

WHAT'S YOUR STORY?

Fritz and Franny can't wait to get ice cream.
Imagine **you** are getting ice cream with Fritz and Franny.
Which ice cream flavor would you want and why?
How many scoops would you get?
Write and draw your story!